ODIN'S FAMILY

ODIN'S FAMILY

MYTHS OF THE VIKINGS

RETOLD BY NEIL PHILIP

ILLUSTRATED BY MARYCLARE FOA

ORCHARD BOOKS
NEW YORK

Orchard Books
95 Madison Avenue
New York, NY 10016

Manufactured in Italy by New Interlitho

10 9 8 7 6 5 4 3 2 1

The text of this book is set in Meridien, with
headings in Trajan.
The illustrations are rendered in oils.

Library of Congress Cataloging-in-Publication Data

Philip, Neil.
Odin's family : myths of the Vikings / retold by Neil Philip;
illustrated by Maryclare Foa. — 1st American ed.
p.   cm.
Includes bibliographical references.
Summary: Retells the myths known by the Vikings, featuring such figures as
Odin, Tyr, Thor, and Frigg.
ISBN 0-531-09531-2
1. Mythology, Norse—Juvenile literature. [1. Mythology, Norse.]
I. Foa, Maryclare, ill. II. Title.
BL860.P45 1996
293'.13—dc20
96–1965

FOR ROWENA AND JOE BIRCH
N.P.

FOR ZIMBABWE AND MOZAMBIQUE
M.F.

CONTENTS

THE CREATION

AT THE BEGINNING OF TIME, nothing was. There was no sand, no sea, no earth, no sky, no growth.

To the north lay the ice realm of Niflheim. To the south, the fires of Muspell. Between Niflheim and Muspell was a nothingness, a gap, a waiting space.

A spring welled up in Niflheim, and from it flowed many rivers, heavy with poison. They flowed into the nothingness, the gap. The poison froze into ice and built up, layer by layer, until the gap was filled.

But just as Niflheim sent its searing winds and sluggish ice flows from the north, so Muspell sent its fiery sparks and dancing airflows from the south. Where the two met, life stirred.

The cold winds from the north and the hot

winds from the south carved the ice into the form of a man. He was Ymir, the father of the frost giants and rock giants.

Ymir slept. And as he slept, he sweated.

Under his left arm a man and woman grew, and from them came others, the first giants.

They lived on the four rivers of milk that flowed from the teats of the cow Audhumla, who was born, like Ymir, from the ice.

Audhumla licked the salty rime itself. She licked ice into man's shape, and that was Buri, the father of the gods.

Buri married Bestla, a frost giant, and they had three sons: Odin, Vili, and Ve. These are the rulers of heaven and earth. Odin is the All-father, the High One.

Odin said to his brothers, "This world should be a place of beauty, not a breeding ground for maggots and monsters." So they slew the sleeping giant Ymir. The blood that gushed from his wounds engulfed the frost giants and rock giants and drowned them all, save the wisest, Bergelmir, who escaped with his family in a hollowed-out tree trunk. Otherwise the whole race of giants would have perished.

Then Odin, Vili, and Ve took Ymir's body and from it fashioned the earth and the sky. The earth was made from his flesh, and the rocks from his bones; the sea that encircles the earth is Ymir's blood. Odin made the sky out of Ymir's skull, and set four dwarfs to hold it up at the four corners. The dwarfs, Durin's people, he bred from the maggots that had infested the giant's slumbering body.

Then Odin shot sparks from Muspell into the sky, to make the stars. And he set the sun and the moon in the sky, and caused the giants Night and Day to drive around the earth every twenty-four hours, in chariots drawn by shining horses.

As Odin and his brothers walked along the new seashore, they came across two driftwood logs. Odin said, "Be." Vili said, "Think." Ve said, "Feel." The logs turned into people. And, greatest gift of all, Odin gave them souls that live and never die, though the body itself has turned to dust.

These two, the first man and the first woman, were named Ask and Embla, after the logs of ash and elm from which they were made.

Odin banished the giants to far Jotunheim and gave the realm of Middle Earth to the race of humans to dwell in.

Odin himself settled in Asgard, which is linked to Middle Earth by the rainbow bridge, Bifrost.

The backbone of all the realms is Yggdrasil, the world tree. Yggdrasil has three great roots. One is in Asgard, home of the gods; one in Jotunheim, home of the giants; and one in dread Niflheim, land of the dead. Beneath the roots the serpent Nidhogg gnaws; at the top of the tree sits an eagle, gazing out with clear, cold eyes over the whole of creation; the squirrel Ratatosk carries insults between the two.

There is a spring beneath each root. The well of wisdom is under the root that is in Jotunheim. Under the root in Niflheim the poison spring that flowed into the gap at the beginning of the world still gurgles its menaces. And in Asgard there is the well of fate, where the gods hold court. There live the three Norns: Urd, Verdandi, and Skuld—Fate, Being, and Necessity. The Norns shape the lives of men and women, from birth to death.

Even the gods cannot escape fate. From the dawning of the world, Surt the fire giant has stood at the gate of fiery Muspell, waiting with his flaming sword for the world to end. Then, in the twilight of the gods, he will wage war against them, and set fire to the whole world.

WAR BETWEEN THE GODS

ODIN LAY WITH THE EARTH HERSELF, and sired red-bearded Thor, the thunderer. Then Odin married Frigg, who knows all fates, but keeps silence about them.

The children of Odin and Frigg were the gods called the Aesir. Thor was the strongest and most straightforward of the gods. When he gave his word, he kept it, and he expected others to keep theirs, too. Whenever the gods needed defending against some threat, they called on Thor.

Balder, Odin's second son, was the fairest and the wisest. Balder shone with an inner brightness that was beautiful to see. His greatest wisdom was his compassion. But because he never thought harm of anyone, Balder was doomed to disappointment.

Others of the Aesir were Tyr, the warrior, and Bragi, the wordsmith; Heimdall, the watchman of the gods, and Ull, the archer; blind Hoder, and Hermod, the messenger; Honir, Odin's companion, and Mimir, the seer.

They lived in Asgard, in the great gold-roofed hall of Gladsheim; there, too, was Valhalla, where Odin receives the souls of warriors slain in battle. The Aesir used so much gold in building Asgard that it shone like a star across the world.

But the Aesir were not the only gods. There were also the children of Vili and Ve, and they were called the Vanir. Chief of them all was Niord, the ruler of the sea, and his children Freyr and Freya, who make the earth fruitful. The Vanir built no great halls, but lived in a misty world woven from spells and magic.

Now the Vanir saw the glistening roofs of Asgard, and their hearts were set on fire with longing for gold. They sent the witch Gullveig to visit their cousins, the Aesir, and see if she could wheedle some gold from them. So Gullveig addressed the gods of Asgard, speaking of red gold, white gold, burning gold—gold, gold, gold, the metal that reflects the heart's desire.

Now Odin was freehanded with gold, as a lord should be. He rewarded many with arm rings and other jewels. He did not hoard his gold, and this greedy, lustful talk of Gullveig's sickened him. So he and the other Aesir took their sharp spears and ran her through, and then they tossed her body on the fire.

But Gullveig could see the past and the future; she knew many things. With her witch's power, she walked unscathed from the fire. Three times they burned her, and three times she came back to life. She returned, empty-handed, to the Vanir.

When the Vanir heard how the Aesir had welcomed Gullveig, they declared war on their cousins. They attacked Asgard with spells, and reduced its walls to rubble. It seemed as if the gods would all kill each other.

At last Odin called to Niord, "Let us declare a truce. Neither of us can defeat the other."

So it was agreed that each side would give hostages to the other, to make sure that the fighting would stop. Niord himself, with Freyr and Freya, went to live with the Aesir, while Honir and Mimir went to the Vanir.

At first everything went well. The Vanir even

made Honir their leader. With Mimir at his side, he always spoke wisely and well. But when Mimir was not there, whenever anyone asked Honir anything at all, he just shrugged his shoulders and said, "Whatever you think best." For Honir was a better drinking companion than he was a ruler of gods.

The Vanir, seeing that they had been tricked into swearing allegiance to a fool, were furious. They seized Mimir and cut off his head, and sent it to Odin with the message that if he didn't know what to do, he could ask Mimir's advice, as that was what Honir always did.

Odin took Mimir's head and cradled it in his arms. In silence, he anointed the head with herbs that would keep it from decay. Then he sang spells over it to give it back the power of speech. And then he followed the Vanir's advice.

Mimir told Odin that there was no future for a world where the gods were at war. As Honir was still the leader of the Vanir, Odin should ask him to join the Vanir to the Aesir so that all the gods could live in peace in Asgard, under Odin's rule.

This is what they did, and to seal the peace all the Aesir and the Vanir spat into a great jar, and

then they fashioned their spittle into a man. His name was Kvasir, and he shared the knowledge and wisdom of every god and every goddess. No one ever asked him a question to which he did not know the answer.

THE WALLS OF ASGARD

AFTER THE CREATION OF KVASIR, the Aesir and the Vanir lived in peace together in Asgard. All the gods were now known as the Aesir.

But there was one other, neither Aesir nor Vanir in origin, who joined their number. His name was Loki, and he was by birth a frost giant, though he had been raised as Odin's foster brother. He was welcomed among the gods because he made them laugh. He was always up to mischief, but he was so quick-witted that he always managed to find some way out of every scrape. So the gods accepted him as one of their own.

If anyone had asked Kvasir if this was wise, they might have received a troubling answer. But no one did ask, and by the time they came to wonder, it was too late.

Loki's wife was called Sigyn, and their son was called Narfi. But he had other children. Among them was Sleipnir, the eight-legged steed of Odin. This is how it happened.

One day there appeared in Asgard a stranger, a builder by trade. He offered to remake the wall that the Vanir had destroyed, and he said that in three seasons he could make it so strong that the rock giants and the frost giants could never destroy it. To make a wall that would withstand the giants was beyond any of the gods, so they listened eagerly to the man's words.

But there was a catch. The stranger said, "As payment for this work, I do not ask for gold." The gods nodded their approval. This man was not another Gullveig, driven by gold-lust. "No," the man repeated, "gold will not satisfy me. Instead, I ask for the goddess Freya to be my wife. Also, I want the sun and moon from the sky."

The gods gasped in horror. After Odin's wife Frigg, Freya was the most powerful of all the goddesses—greater than Eir, the healer, or Gefion, the maiden; more passionate than Siofn or Lofn, the goddesses of love; and wiser than Var, the oath taker, or Vor, the guide. Freya wore one of

the great treasures of the world, the necklace Brisingamen, but she herself was a greater treasure to the Aesir. They did not like to think of her married to a mere builder, no longer free to ride out in war or peace in her chariot pulled by two wildcats. They murmured, "No, no."

But Loki said, "Do not be hasty. Let's shorten the time. If this stranger can build his wall in one winter, let him have Freya for his bride. If not, he gets nothing, and we get at least part of a wall."

The gods agreed, for surely no one man could possibly fulfill such a task.

The builder accepted the new terms, only asking to be allowed to have the help of his stallion, Svadilfari.

"Why not?" said Loki, and the gods once more agreed. They swore great oaths to bind them to the contract.

Soon they began to regret listening to Loki. For the stranger worked with ferocious energy. Every day he spent building the wall, and every night he went with Svadilfari to fetch more stone. Without the horse, he would have been lost, but with it, he made great progress.

With three days left before summer, the wall

was very nearly finished. The gods were beside themselves with misery and worry, and began to cast around for someone to blame.

"It is your fault, Loki," said Odin. "Soon the sky will be darkened forever, and bright-eyed Freya will be lost to us. You must find a way to stop it."

Loki said, "Don't worry. I will stop this builder in his tracks, whatever it takes." But he would not tell the other gods his plan.

That night, as the builder led Svadilfari down to the quarry to fetch more stone, a beautiful mare appeared at the edge of the wood and whinnied at the stallion. Then it turned into the wood and cantered off. Svadilfari, maddened by the sight and scent of this lovely creature, pulled free from his master and plunged into the wood in pursuit. And though the builder called and called, the stallion did not come back.

The next day the builder scarcely got any work done at all, and soon it became clear that he would never finish the wall. He knew that he had been tricked, but he did not know how. So all he could do was fly into a terrible rage. He filled himself with so much anger that he swelled out into his true, giant shape. And when the gods saw that he

was indeed a rock giant, they determined that he must die. Thor struck the giant on the head, crushing his skull into fragments.

And some weeks after that, Loki returned to Asgard. He was riding a foal, as gangly and skittish as any other, but different in one respect: It had eight legs. For while its father was the stallion Svadilfari, its mother was the shape-changing trickster Loki.

Loki wasn't ashamed; he was smirking at his own cleverness. He just said, "I told you that giant would never finish his wall."

As for the eight-legged foal, Odin named him Sleipnir and took him for his steed. Sleipnir would carry the All-father anywhere, even down to the realms of the dead.

THE TREASURES OF
THE GODS

WITH HIS GREAT RED BEARD, his blustery manner, and his huge appetite, the thunder god Thor was someone to reckon with. But unlike battle-thirsty Odin, or the warrior god Tyr, or even Freya, who claimed her own tribute of souls from the battlefield, Thor did not like fighting. He also didn't like being made a fool of.

The great love of Thor's life was his wife, Sif, with her lovely golden hair. Thor said it reminded him of a field of grain, waving in the breeze.

So when Loki, who was bored and looking for fun, cut off Sif's hair, Thor couldn't see the joke. He pinned Loki up against a door and reminded him that the humans down in Middle Earth sometimes pinned their enemies like that, and left them hanging with their rib cages splayed open.

31

"If you're really bored, we could introduce the custom to Asgard."

Loki didn't think that was funny at all. "There's no need for that," he said. "I'll replace Sif's hair. I'll get the dwarfs to forge her new hair, out of real gold. It will be better than ever."

So Loki went to the dwarfs Brokk and Eitri to ask them to make new hair for Sif. But he didn't have any way of paying for such a treasure. So he didn't ask directly. Instead, he described all kinds of wonderful things to them, making them up as he went along, and every time he ended, "That's just the kind of thing we need in Asgard. But, of course, you couldn't make something like it. I'd bet my head on it."

The two dwarfs began to argue about what could and couldn't be done. "Well," said Loki, "which of you is the better craftsman?"

"Me!" said Brokk and Eitri at the same time.

So Loki said, "If you each make the three best pieces you can and bring them to Asgard, the gods will judge which of you is the finer smith."

Brokk and Eitri, who were brothers, didn't need any more encouragement than that. They set to work with a will.

Brokk made the new hair for Sif. Then he made a spear, named Gungnir, that would pierce any target. Then he made a ship, called Skidbladnir, that could be folded up like cloth and kept in a pocket. And then he stood back, and said, "Match that!"

Eitri took his turn. He put a pig's hide in the forge, and told his brother to work the bellows and not let up whatever happened. A horsefly settled on Brokk's arm and bit him, but he carried on blowing, and when Eitri took his work out of the forge, it had turned into a boar with bristles of real gold. It could travel by sky or sea faster than a galloping horse, and its bristles gave out their own light in the dark.

Then Eitri put gold in the forge, and once again told Brokk to work the bellows without a pause. The fly came back and bit Brokk's neck, but he carried on blowing, and when Eitri took his work out of the forge, it was a gold arm ring, named Draupnir. Every ninth night, it shed eight other rings of the same size.

Then Eitri put iron in the forge. This time the fly settled between Brokk's eyes and bit him until the blood ran into them. He took one hand off the bellows to swipe the fly away.

When Eitri's third piece came out of the forge, it was a hammer—the greatest hammer ever made. It would crush anything it struck, and never miss a target if it was thrown, and never fly so far that it could not be found. But it was not perfect. Because Brokk had taken his hand from the bellows, the handle was slightly short.

Whether the fly was Loki, or just a fly, no one knows.

The two dwarfs took their treasures to Asgard and showed them proudly to the gods. Odin, Thor, and Freyr were to be the judges.

Brokk gave the golden hair to Thor for poor, bald Sif, and the spear Gungnir to Odin, and the folding ship Skidbladnir to Freyr. And Eitri gave the boar with the golden bristles to Freyr, and the ring Draupnir to Odin, and the short-handled hammer to Thor.

The gods thought long and hard about their judgment, and eventually they decided that, despite its short handle, Thor's hammer, Miollnir, was the finest piece of work.

"Well done, Eitri," they said. "You are the best."

"That's wonderful," said Eitri. "And now, what about our payment?"

"What payment?" said Odin. "We never asked you to give us these wonderful gifts. We have paid you by choosing between you."

So Eitri, seeing how he had been cheated by Loki, said, "That's all very well. The gods may not pay us for our smithwork, but will they make Loki here keep his word?"

"What do you mean?" asked Thor.

"When Loki challenged us to make these things, he bet his head that we could not do it. If I am not going to be paid with gold, I want to be paid with Loki's head."

Loki tried to run, but Thor caught him, and brought him struggling back. "We gods of Asgard keep our word," he said.

The dwarf took a blade and prepared to cut off Loki's head. He tested the blade's edge with his finger, and whistled through his teeth as he swung it back.

"Stop! Stop!" shouted Loki. "My head may be yours, but no one said anything about the neck. I'll thank you to leave that alone."

So Eitri was thwarted of his revenge. But before he left, he sewed up Loki's lips with a leather thong, and it was a long time before Loki managed to get them untied.

None of the gods would help him. "It serves him right," said Thor.

"And it gives us some peace and quiet," said Sif, gently shaking her new hair, which lay across her shoulders like liquid gold.

ODIN'S WISDOM

WHEN ODIN SAT IN HIS HIGH THRONE IN ASGARD, he could see the whole world and everything in it. And because he wanted to know all things, he sent his two ravens, Huginn and Muninn, to crisscross the world and come back each evening to whisper into his ears the secrets of the world. In truth these ravens are the thoughts of Odin, flying with their dark wings and fierce bright eyes across the skies of his creation.

Other than the golden apples of life, which kept the gods young, Odin required no food. But nevertheless he hungered. Knowledge was the food and drink he needed. To gain it, he even left one of his eyes in the well of wisdom, beneath the world tree Yggdrasil, in return for one sip of its water. It was in that well that he placed the

severed head of Mimir, so that the seer could drink from it every day.

Still Odin wanted more. He wanted to know everything that was, that is, that will be.

So one day Odin went alone to Yggdrasil, the great ash tree that is the pillar of all the worlds.

Odin lashed himself to the trunk of the tree, and pierced himself through with a spear. Nine nights he hung there to earn the knowledge of the runes that contain the secrets of the world.

For nine nights he suffered in torment. And at last there came a moment when he could see through his pain. He looked up and, with a cry, seized the magic runes from the boughs of Yggdrasil.

Men and women could use runes to write down words; Odin the All-father used them to bend the world to his will. With the spell-runes, he grew great in wisdom. He could help any sorrow, cure any illness, escape any trap, vanquish any enemy. He could walk through fire and feel no burning; he could lure any girl into his arms.

All this, Odin learned upon the tree of life.

THE MEAD OF POETRY

EVEN WITH ALL THEIR WISDOM AND POWER, the gods were not safe from treachery and lies. Not even wise Kvasir, who was made from the spittle of every god and every goddess.

When Kvasir was on his travels about the world, he stayed one night as the guest of two dwarfs, Fialar and Galar.

As he talked to them, Kvasir revealed more and more of his knowledge and wisdom. As words of insight dropped from his lips, Fialar and Galar exchanged a glance.

Then Fialar said, "Come into the back room for a moment. There's something we'd like your opinion on."

Kvasir went with them into the back, and there they showed him a great cauldron standing empty.

40

"In this cauldron," said Galar, "we intend to brew a mead of poetry. We will stir in honey so that the words will taste sweet in the poet's mouth, but we need some other ingredient."

"Well," said Kvasir, "I would say that you need something that will give meaning to the words and make them pulse with life."

"Our thoughts exactly," said Fialar, and he and Galar drew their knives and stabbed Kvasir to death.

They drained his blood into the cauldron, mixed it with honey, and brewed the mead of poetry. They did not offer it to others, but kept it in secret for themselves alone, as is the way of dwarfs.

They might have kept it forever, had they not invited a giant called Gilling and his wife to stay with them. Dwarfs and giants have never been able to get along, and soon Fialar and Galar hated Gilling more than anyone in the world. So they asked him to go fishing with them and, when they were out at sea, pushed him overboard and drowned him.

When they told Gilling's wife about his sad end, they were full of sympathy. "It's such a shame," said Galar, "that he couldn't swim."

Then Fialar said, "Come outside with me, and we will look out to sea. It will be a comfort to you." So Gilling's wife went and stood outside the dwarfs' doorway, gazing out over the ocean where her husband had come to grief.

While she stood there, Fialar sent Galar onto the roof with a millstone, and Galar dropped it on her head and killed her, too.

Now, Gilling and his wife had a son, named Suttung, and when they did not return home, he came looking for them. Fialar and Galar told him with very long faces how sad they were that both of his parents should have come to such untimely, accidental deaths, but Suttung didn't believe a word they said. So he took them down to the sea, one beneath each arm, and tied them to a rock below the high-water level. Then, as the tide came in, he asked them again how his parents had died.

The dwarfs soon confessed it all, and Suttung was of a mind to leave them there to die. But they begged and pleaded, and at last they offered him the precious mead in exchange for their lives.

So Fialar and Galar went free, and Suttung took the mead back to Jotunheim, where he hid it inside a mountain, with his daughter Gunnlod guarding it.

The gods hadn't really missed Kvasir; he was always wandering around the world. But when they heard the story of Suttung and the dwarfs, they determined that, even if they couldn't bring Kvasir back to life, at least they would possess the mead of poetry that had been brewed from his blood.

So Odin set out for Jotunheim. He didn't have to wear a disguise. He just had to think differently, and he looked different. This time he called himself Bolverk.

As Bolverk, Odin went to see a giant called Baugi, who was Suttung's brother, and offered to work for him for a whole summer for no pay other than a single sip of Suttung's mead. "I'll do the work of nine men," he said.

Baugi replied that the mead was Suttung's. "I'll ask him on your behalf, but I can't promise he'll agree."

So Bolverk worked for Baugi all summer, doing the work of nine men, and when winter came they went to see Suttung and explained their agreement.

"You must be joking," said Suttung. "I don't care if you did the work of a hundred men. You're not getting so much as a taste of my mead."

That put Baugi in a spot. Bolverk had worked so hard, it seemed wrong to deny him his sip of mead.

Bolverk said, "If Suttung won't give me the mead, we must find some other way."

"What other way?" said Baugi. "The mead is hidden in a chamber in the heart of the mountain, and even if you could get in there, Gunnlod is guarding it day and night. There's no chance."

"Well," said Bolverk, "if there's no chance, there's no harm in trying." He handed Baugi a drill, over which he had muttered runes, and told him, "See if you can bore through the mountain with that."

Baugi started to drill, and after a while he said, "I've got all the way through."

Bolverk blew into the hole, and chippings flew back into his face. "Try again," he said.

So Baugi went back to work, and this time when Bolverk blew down the hole, the chippings blew out the other side, and he knew that the hole went all the way through to the hidden chamber.

Then Odin stopped being Bolverk and turned into a snake. As he slipped into the hole, Baugi hit out at him with the drill, but Odin was too fast. He slithered all the way down to where Gunnlod sat on her golden chair, keeping her lonely guard over the precious mead.

Then Odin turned back into Bolverk—a one-eyed, handsome giant of a man. He said, "I have come to keep you company. I could not bear to think of one so beautiful sitting alone in the mountain, with no one to talk to, no one to cuddle, no one to kiss." And he put his arms around Gunnlod and kissed her full on the lips.

No woman could resist Odin. Gunnlod embraced him with all the slow-burning passion of her proud spirit.

Then she said, "What can I give you in return for your love?"

Odin replied, "Give me three sips of your father's mead."

Gunnlod agreed, and with three enormous sips Odin emptied the cauldron. Then he slithered back through the drill-hole and, turning into an eagle, flew back to Asgard.

Suttung pursued him, also in eagle form. As

Odin crossed the wall of Asgard, Suttung was right behind him. But no giant could pass the wall that the rock giant had built in hopes of winning Freya for his wife. Suttung screamed in frustration and wheeled back to Jotunheim.

As he flew in, Odin spat the mead into bowls that the gods had laid out in the yard. But some spilled outside the walls of Asgard. The gods said that anyone who wanted that could have it, and it is known as the rhymer's share. Even the plainest of people sometimes get a taste of it.

The rest the gods kept. But Odin sometimes grants a sip of inspiration to men and women, blessing and cursing them with the gift of poetry.

THE APPLES OF LIFE

THE GODS NEVER GREW OLD, for each day they fed on the ever-renewing apples of life. These were in the safekeeping of Idun, the wife of Bragi, the god to whom Odin entrusted the mead of poetry.

The gods never thought about what they would do if those precious apples were ever lost or stolen. They were always young, and they had the happy confidence of youth.

It was in just such a carefree mood that Odin, Loki, and Honir set out one day on a cross-country jaunt. They walked until they were exhausted. So when they saw a herd of oxen, they didn't think twice before slaughtering one and making an earth oven to cook it in.

Loki and Honir were very hungry after so much exercise, and so they waited eagerly for the food to be ready. But though the flames licked all around it, it would not cook. They argued among themselves about what could be wrong, but they just couldn't understand it.

Then they heard a voice from the oak tree above them. "It's my doing," the voice said.

They looked up and saw an enormous eagle perched in the branches of the tree. It said, "If you let me eat my fill of the ox, I will let it cook." And they agreed.

However, when starving Loki saw the bird begin to devour the entire beast, he struck out angrily at it with his staff.

The staff stuck to the eagle's body, and the bird rose into the air, carrying Loki with it. He found he couldn't let go. There was nothing he could do but hang on, though the eagle flew so low that he got a terrible buffeting from rocks and branches on the way. However Loki begged, the eagle would not let him go.

"I'll do anything! Anything!" he screamed.

"Anything?" said the eagle.

"Yes, yes! Anything!" cried the desperate Loki.

"If you promise to bring me Idun and the apples of life," said the eagle, "I will let you go."

And Loki promised.

When Loki rejoined Odin and Honir, he let them make fun of his tattered and bedraggled condition, but he did not tell them of his promise to the eagle. He just said, "Let's go back to Asgard."

When they reached Asgard, Loki went to see Idun. He said, "You've probably heard that I was carried off by a huge eagle. Everyone thinks it's a great joke. But the thing is, while it was dragging me along, I saw the most wonderful thing. It was an apple tree, groaning with apples. I promise you, they looked twice as big and twice as luscious as those apples of yours. You would love them!"

"No apples could rival mine," said Idun.

"If you don't believe me, come and see for yourself," said Loki. "And bring your apples with you, so we can compare them."

So Idun went into the forest with Loki, and once she was there the eagle snatched her up in its claws and carried her and the apples of life away to Jotunheim. For the eagle was really the giant Thiassi. Loki had kept his promise.

Next morning, Odin woke up with a pain in his hip. Frigg found some white hairs. Freyr felt oddly tired; Freya didn't get up at all.

Soon all the gods were suffering from aches and pains. They started to lose their hair and walk stiffly and forget what they had been meaning to say. They started to grow old.

Odin called a council. "What has happened to Idun?" he asked, though the voice that once rang like thunder was now weak and trembling. "Someone must know."

"I saw her go into the forest with Loki," said Heimdall, the gods' watchman. By day or night he can see for a hundred miles. He can hear the grass grow. He needs less sleep than a bird; but even he was tired that day.

"Loki!" said Odin with disgust. "I might have known. Bring him to me!"

The gods had to drag Loki kicking and screaming to the well of fate.

"Where is Idun?" asked Odin.

Loki did not reply.

"Where is she?"

Loki looked away.

"Tell us!"

"Well," said Loki, "you remember that eagle..."

"Get on with it!"

"The eagle was the giant Thiassi. He has Idun,

and her apples."

Thor began to finger his great hammer, Miollnir.

"I'll get her back, I promise," yelped Loki. He turned to Freya. "Will you lend me your falcon skin?"

After the necklace Brisingamen, this was Freya's most precious possession. With it she could fly right into the otherworld. But what use to her was her falcon skin when she felt so feeble? She let Loki borrow the skin.

So it was in falcon form that Loki flew to Jotunheim. He found Idun in Thiassi's garden; the giant himself was out fishing. Idun was no longer the merry girl Loki had known in Asgard. Grief had worn lines into her face, like the lines of age that were disfiguring the other gods. She was cradling the precious apples in her apron.

Loki used his own magic to turn her into a nut. He picked her up in his claws and flew back to Asgard as fast as he could.

Thiassi was not far behind, in his eagle shape. And, over distance, the eagle can outfly the falcon.

Loki felt the giant gaining on him. He flapped his wings so hard that he seemed to be riding a storm.

Heimdall saw him coming from miles away, and the gods prepared a great pile of wood shavings outside the walls of Asgard. As soon as Loki passed overhead, they lit a fire.

The flames shot up and caught Thiassi in their searing heat. With his eagle feathers burned away, he returned to giant shape, and the gods slew him where he lay.

Then gentle Idun handed out apples of life to the gods—even to two-faced Loki—and, as they ate, the lines fell from their faces, and the spring came back into their steps.

THIASSI'S DAUGHTER

THE ROCK GIANT THIASSI HAD A DAUGHTER, named Skadi. When he did not return, she put on helmet and coat of mail, and took up her father's weapons, and went to Asgard to the well of fate.

She stood before the gods and said, "I am one and you are many. I know that you can kill me, just as you killed my father. So if you will not give me justice, give me death."

Odin's heart was touched by her bravery. "We cannot bring Thiassi back to life," he said. "But we will grant you three wishes, or be shamed before the world."

"This is my first wish," said Skadi. "I want the god of my choice as my husband."

The gods grimaced, but agreed.

"This is my second wish," she said. "I want

you to make me laugh." And she looked at them with a face so stern and sad that their hearts quailed.

"And this is my third and last wish. As you cannot bring my father back to life, I want you to make him immortal."

Odin replied, "Your third wish is the easiest." And he took Thiassi's eyes and threw them into the sky, to live forever as stars.

"Your second wish," said Odin, "is more difficult."

But while Odin was speaking, Loki was moving. He took a length of string and tied one end around the beard of Thor's nanny goat and the other end around his own hair. Whenever one of them moved, the other shrieked.

"Save me! Save me!" cried Loki, and with a final heartrending scream he leaped into Skadi's arms, and hung there with his arms around her neck, looking piteously into her eyes. She couldn't help it. Despite herself, she dissolved into helpless laughter.

"Now there is only one wish to fulfill," said Odin. "You shall have your choice of husband, but you shall choose from the feet alone."

All the gods of Asgard, even Odin himself, stood

in a line, covered with material so that only their feet showed.

Skadi went up and down the line, trying to guess who was who. She had her mind set on Balder, the most perfect of all the gods.

One pair of feet was particularly beautiful. "These must be Balder's," she said. "I choose you."

But it was not Balder. It was Niord, the father of Freyr and Freya.

So Skadi married Niord.

The two of them could not agree about anything. Niord said, "I must be near the sea."

Skadi said, "I must live in the mountains."

They agreed to live nine nights in the mountains and nine nights by the sea, turn and turn about. But after the first nine nights in the mountains Niord said, "Never again! I couldn't get a wink of sleep, with all those howling wolves."

And after the first nine nights by the sea, Skadi said, "I can't bear it! The screaming of those gulls will drive me mad."

So Skadi lived in the mountains, and Niord lived by the sea, with only the restless winds to carry messages between them.

THOR'S HAMMER

ONE DAY, THOR LOOKED FOR HIS hammer Miollnir but could not find it anywhere. It was gone.

Thor's thunderous roaring could be heard across the skies of all the worlds. "Where is my hammer?"

His first thought was that Loki must have taken it, but Loki swore he had not touched it. "Let me search for it," said the crafty god. "Some giant may have stolen it. If Freya will lend me her falcon skin again, I can be back in no time at all."

So Loki flew off in falcon shape, to Jotunheim where the giants lived. There he found a giant named Thrym, sitting on a mound.

"I've been expecting you," said Thrym. "I suppose you've come for Thor's hammer."

Loki could only stutter in reply.

"You can have it if you like," Thrym continued.

"It's no use to me. I've just buried it way under the ground. I don't intend to use it. But of course there's a price."

"We'll pay anything," said Loki, for the gods had come to rely on Thor's hammer as their best defense against the giants.

"In that case," said Thrym, "you can send me the goddess Freya to be my bride."

Loki flew back to Asgard, to a cool reception from the gods. They were inclined to blame him for the whole affair.

"Do you think we saved Freya from the giant who built our wall just to give her away to Thrym?" asked Odin. "We'll have to find another way."

"He wouldn't make such a bad husband," said Loki, "once you'd got used to the smell."

"Don't even think of it," said Freya.

"In that case," said Loki, "there's only one thing to do." He turned to Sif. "Do you still have your bridal veil and gown?"

"Of course."

"Then bring them here."

When Sif returned, Loki took the clothes from her, and said, "Thor, just stand still for a moment."

And then Loki carefully dressed the red-bearded thunder god as a blushing bride.

Sif thought it was the funniest thing she had ever seen.

Thor looked very uncomfortable. He said, "A joke's a joke, Loki. But no giant would ever be fooled by this."

"I don't know," said Loki, "in a half-light, you look very fetching. I could marry you myself." And Loki lifted Thor's veil and planted a kiss on his cheek.

So Thor set out for Jotunheim, with Loki dressed as his maid.

When they arrived, the giant Thrym was overcome with delight and arranged the wedding for that very evening.

At the wedding feast, Thor sat in his bridal gown at the women's end of the table. The women were picking listlessly at the dainties reserved for them. Thor polished off a whole ox and eight salmon, and washed them down with a lake of mead.

Thrym said, "Freya certainly likes her food."

Loki the maid leaned across the table and whispered, "She is a woman of prodigious appetites."

Thrym shivered in anticipation.

Then Thrym called for Thor's hammer Miollnir to be brought forward, for all weddings and funerals must be blessed with a hammer.

"Lay the hammer on Freya's lap," said Thrym, "and wish us joy together."

They put the hammer on Thor's lap, and Thrym raised the veil for a kiss. But he fell back in dismay at the burning light in his bride's eyes.

Then Thor lifted the hammer, and struck Thrym dead.

Thor and Loki journeyed back to Asgard in high spirits, and Thor never let the hammer out of his sight again.

THOR AND LOKI AMONG THE GIANTS

EVEN GODS CAN GET BORED. One day, Loki could bear it no longer. "Nothing ever happens in this place!" he shouted. "All this peace and quiet is driving me mad."

"It must be a change for you," said Sif sweetly, "not to have anyone wanting to cut off your head."

"Is that all the thanks I get," asked Loki, "for getting you that beautiful hair, and helping Thor here to win back his hammer?" He put on a ludicrous expression of mock hurt.

Thor laughed his great rumbling laugh. "You're right, Loki. I do owe you for that. So what do you want to do?"

"Let's go and tease the giants in Jotunheim," said Loki. "I feel like an adventure."

"Your adventures always turn into disasters," said Sif.

But Thor said, "Boredom is worse than danger. Let's go!"

They set off in Thor's chariot, drawn by his two goats, Tanngniost and Tanngrisnir. In the evening they came to a farmhouse, and asked for a night's lodging.

It was a poor place. But the earth floor was clean enough and covered with fresh rushes. A fire was burning in the hearth. The farmer, burly and tanned with short brown hair and a neatly trimmed beard, was sitting on a stool in his thonged shirt, carving wood. His wife was sitting by him, spinning yarn, her shawl neatly fastened over her long dress with a bronze brooch. When she saw the gods, she rose to her feet, stammering that while "Your Lordships" were of course welcome, she had very little to offer them: just a loaf of unleavened bread made from bran.

"Don't worry about that," said Thor. "We can feed ourselves."

That evening, Thor slaughtered his goats, skinned them, and boiled them over the fire. Then he beckoned to the farmer and his wife and their two children, "Come, eat. There's enough for all."

He carefully placed the goatskins to one side of the fire, and said, "Be sure to put all the bones on the skins. I'll need them later."

They all sat down to eat. It was a delicious meal, the best that the poor family had eaten for a long while. It was so good that, while Thor wasn't looking, the farmer's son, Thialfi, couldn't resist breaking open a thighbone to get at the delicious marrow inside. Then he threw the broken bone onto the skin with the rest.

At dawn, Thor rose. He shook Loki awake. "It's time we were on our way," he said. Then he took his hammer, Miollnir, and blessed the goatskins. Tanngniost got up as if nothing had happened, but Tanngrisnir was limping. Thor saw at once that its leg was broken.

Thor's shout of fury made the house walls tremble. The poor farmer cast himself onto the floor in terror. Thor's voice was the growl of a coming storm. "You shall pay for this!" His knuckles whitened around his hammer.

But when he saw the man cowering in fear, Thor's anger calmed. He agreed to accept the son, Thialfi, and the daughter, Roskva, as his bond servants, in payment of the debt. "I will leave the goats here, and expect to find them well when I return," he said.

"But where are we going?" asked Roskva.

"Why, to Jotunheim, of course," said Loki. The mischief maker wanted to see the girl go pale with fright. But she was a spirited lass.

"That's quite a distance," she said. "So the sooner we leave, the sooner we'll get there."

With that, the party set out on its way to the east.

They reached the sea that separates Middle Earth from Jotunheim, and crossed it in a fishing boat. The waves were so lively that Loki was sick over the side. "I wish I were a mortal," he moaned, "so that I could die right now." But at last they came to the shore.

As they ventured inland they came to a huge forest. Thor sent Thialfi running ahead to look for somewhere they could stay for the night, but there was no dwelling. It grew dark, and they still had no lodging.

Then they came to a huge building standing empty. It had a single entrance as wide as the whole building, and they sheltered just inside it. At midnight there was an earthquake. The ground shuddered beneath them, and they didn't feel at all safe. They hardly dared sneeze, they were so anxious. So they moved into a side chamber that led off to the right about halfway down the building. All night long the ground trembled with aftershocks.

When dawn came, they went back out into the forest. There, lying fast asleep, was the source of all the tremors: a giant, snoring in great stertorous gasps that shook the whole forest. Thor took his hammer, ready to strike, but at that moment the giant awoke, and Thor, weary from a night without sleep, held his blow.

Instead he asked meekly, "What is your name?"

The giant answered, "My name is Skrymir," which means "Big Lad" in the tongue of the giants. "I don't need to ask your name. You must be Thor of the Aesir, with that beard and that hammer. But what have you been doing with my glove?"

Then Skrymir bent down and picked up his glove, which was the building in which Thor and his companions had spent the night. The side-chamber was the thumb of the glove. Thor had never felt such a fool in all his days.

Then Skrymir undid his knapsack and brought

out food for his breakfast. "You're welcome to join me," he said. "If you like, we can journey together awhile, and pool our provisions. I'll carry everything." Thor agreed.

After breakfast, they put all their food into Skrymir's knapsack, and he tied it up. Then he strode ahead through the forest, and the others tried to keep up with him—but he had such long legs, it was impossible. By the time they caught up with him, it was late in the evening.

Skrymir was spread out under an oak tree. "I've already eaten," he said, "and now I'm ready to sleep. Just help yourself from the knapsack." He closed his eyes and at once began to snore. It sounded like a herd of cows who haven't been milked.

Thor took the knapsack and tried to open it, but he couldn't so much as loosen a single strap. When he realized that after a long day's forced march he wasn't going to get any supper, he flew into a temper. He grasped Miollnir, and swung the terrible hammer with all his strength at Skrymir's head.

The giant stirred in his sleep. "Did a leaf fall on me?" he mumbled.

When the giant was fast asleep again, Thor struck him once more. He felt Miollnir sinking deep into the giant's forehead.

Yet once again, Skrymir only surfaced to say, "Was that an acorn?" before returning to his slumbers.

As dawn approached, Thor and his companions were feeling quite desperate. They had had no sleep for two nights. They had no food. And they could not keep up with Skrymir's pace.

Thor decided to strike again. This time, he strained every muscle in his body to deliver a crushing blow. He buried Miollnir right up to its handle in the giant's head.

This time, Skrymir did wake. He rubbed at his forehead, saying, "Is there a bird up in the tree? I'm sure I felt its droppings on my head."

Seeing that Thor and his companions were already up, Skrymir said, "There's no need to bother with breakfast this morning. We're not far from the fortress of Utgard, and you can get something to eat there. Just head east. But I warn you, I'm a stripling compared with the brawny fellows that live there. I wouldn't get too cocky with them if I were you—they won't put up with

it. I can't come with you; I have business in the north. Good-bye!"

As Skrymir strode off, Thor, Loki, Thialfi, and Roskva waved and shouted, "Good-bye! Good-bye!"

"And good riddance," added Loki when the giant was out of hearing.

Then they set off eastward toward the fortress of Utgard.

The fortress stood on open ground. It towered into the sky, so that they had to crane their necks to see over it. There was a gate across the entrance, and it was shut tight. No one answered their shouts, so Thor tugged and pulled at the gate, but he couldn't get it open.

Eventually they got inside by squeezing through the bars. They went up to the great hall and, as the door was standing open, walked in. There were many giants inside, sitting on two benches. At their head was their king, Utgard-Loki.

For several moments no one noticed the intruders. Then Utgard-Loki bared his teeth in a savage grin and said, "What have we here? Surely this puny specimen can't be the great Thor that we've heard so much about? Though, it's true, gossip does tend to exaggerate."

"I am Thor," said the god through gritted teeth.

"Well, well, well. Perhaps you're stronger than you look." Utgard-Loki gave a silky smile, and the rows of giants sniggered. Thor went red in the face.

"Anyway," said Utgard-Loki, "you are welcome here, and your companions. That is, as long as each of you has some skill at which you are a champion. No one can visit this castle without testing themselves against us."

Then Loki spoke. "There is something I can do better than anyone else."

"And what is that?"

"Eat!" replied Loki, who was starving, what with being sick on the boat and hardly eating a thing since. "I'll match myself against anyone in the world in an eating contest."

Utgard-Loki clapped his hands, and servants scurried to and fro. They dragged a huge wooden trencher into the middle of the hall and piled it high with meat. A giant named Logi was summoned to be the giants' champion.

Loki sat down at one end, and Logi at the other. At the signal, they both started to guzzle their way along the trencher. Loki ate like a ravening animal, using his teeth to tear the meat from the bones and devouring the gobbets whole. The juices dripping down his chin made him look like a monster from a nightmare. Logi, too, ate with astonishing speed.

Loki and Logi met exactly halfway. They were so intent on eating that they didn't know what was happening until they crashed heads. Loki reeled dazed onto the floor, sat up, let out a satisfied belch, and looked blearily at Utgard-Loki.

"You haven't done badly, for a small fry," said the giant-king, "but you're such an untidy eater."

"What do you mean?" shouted Loki. "I haven't left a scrap."

While it was true that Loki had left a terrible mess of bones behind him, he had eaten all the meat. But when he looked to the other end, he could see that Logi had eaten not just the meat, but the bones and even the trencher as well. Loki had to admit defeat.

"What next?" said Utgard-Loki.

Thialfi piped up, "I can run fast." So they went outside and set up a race between Thialfi and a giant named Hugi.

They set off, but by the time Thialfi found his

stride, Hugi had completed the course and run back to meet him halfway.

"Well, I'm sure you did your best, lad," said Utgard-Loki, and patted Thialfi on the head as they returned to the hall.

Then the giant-king leered at Roskva. "And what can you do?" he asked.

"I can look after myself," said Roskva. And Utgard-Loki had no answer to that.

So the giant-king turned at last to Thor, the thunderer. "And you, little fellow," he said, "what will you do?"

Thor replied. "I am reckoned a great drinker, among the gods."

"Among the gods, eh?" chuckled Utgard-Loki, and all the giants laughed as if he had cracked the funniest joke they'd ever heard.

Utgard-Loki commanded a drinking horn to be brought forward. "This is the horn we drink from," he said. "The best of us can drain it in one swig, most of us in two; no one is so feeble they can't empty it in three goes."

It was a big horn, and it did seem rather long, but Thor was very thirsty. He had no doubt he could manage it. He began to gulp down the drink, and continued until he ran out of breath. When he looked in the horn, he had scarcely made any difference. So he took a second enormous gulp, but still only lowered the level slightly. For the third swig, he kept going until he nearly passed out. When he looked, he had made a good inroad into the horn, but it was still half full.

"As I said," remarked Utgard-Loki, "gossip does exaggerate. I was a fool to believe all those stories about the great Thor. You're obviously not as tough as they say."

Thor said, "I am reckoned tough by the gods."

All the giants laughed again.

Utgard-Loki replied, "In that case, let me suggest a game of some of our youngsters. It's silly, really. All they do is lift my cat off the floor. It's child's play."

The cat was a huge creature. Thor picked it up by the belly and pulled. It arched its back, and Thor thrust up with all his strength, until he was standing at full stretch. He strained every nerve, and the cat lifted one paw off the ground. But he could do no more.

"Well," said Utgard-Loki, "it is a big cat."

Thor was beside himself with anger—as full

of fury as one of the wild berserks, whom Odin fills with battle rage. "I'll take on any one of you with my bare hands," he shouted. "Come and fight!"

"Temper, temper," said Utgard-Loki. "I really don't think any of us giants should lower ourselves so far as to fight someone who can't even pick up the cat."

Thor growled.

"Let me think," said Utgard-Loki. "I have it. You can fight Elli, my old nurse. She should be a match for you."

A withered old crone hobbled into the hall and struck up a wrestling pose.

Thor fought her with all his strength. But however he struggled, he could not budge the old woman. Worse, he felt himself being gradually overcome. At last, Elli forced him down onto one knee.

"Stop the fight! Stop the fight!" shouted Utgard-Loki. "It's useless to continue, if you can't even hold your ground against an old woman."

So Thor and his companions retired to bed, sore and unhappy.

The next morning they were given a handsome

breakfast, and Utgard-Loki himself offered to see them on their way.

Once they were clear of the fortress, Utgard-Loki said, "I hope you enjoyed your visit."

"No, I did not," Thor replied, "for I was made to look a fool and a weakling."

"Not so," said Utgard-Loki. "You should know that I am Skrymir, the giant you met in the forest. Look over there, and you will see three square-shaped valleys. They were not there before. They are the marks made by the blows of your hammer. If I had not put that mountain between myself and your hammer, I would never have survived.

"I tried to weaken you by depriving you of food, for I knew you could never undo my rucksack. But if I had known then the strength you have in you, I would never have allowed you into my fortress. You were nearly the ruin of me, the lot of you.

"You, Loki, were the first to accept my challenge to perform some feat of strength and skill. You matched Logi in speed and hunger, but you could never beat him. For he is Flame, the wildfire that consumes everything in its path.

"Then you, Thialfi, matched yourself against Hugi. But he is Thought, and you could never run as fast as him.

"You, Roskva, put up with no nonsense. As we giants say, 'Never tangle with a quick-witted woman.'

"And Thor, when you were drinking from the horn, I thought my heart would stop. For the other end of that horn was in the sea, and I thought you would drain the ocean dry.

"As for the cat, how you lifted even a paw is a mystery, for that cat was Jormungand, the world serpent that encircles the earth with its tail in its mouth. You stretched it nearly to the sky.

"But the greatest of all your feats was the wrestling match. For Elli is no other than Old Age, and she could only bring you to one knee. There never has been anyone, and there never will be anyone, whom Old Age cannot overcome."

When Thor heard how he and his companions had been duped, he reached for his hammer. But as he swung it through the air, Utgard-Loki disappeared. And when Thor looked back at the fortress, it was gone, too. All that remained was a level, empty plain, shimmering in the sun.

So Thor, Loki, Thialfi, and Roskva made their way back to Asgard from the land of the giants.

Since Thor's drinking bout, the ocean shrinks and swells twice a day, remembering the time the thunder god nearly drank it dry.

LOKI'S CHILDREN

LOKI THE TRICKSTER was the father of Narfi by his wife Sigyn, and the mother of Sleipnir by the stallion Svadilfari. But he also had three other children, loathsome creatures he fathered with the giantess Angrboda, before he ever came to Asgard.

The first of these was Jormungand, the world serpent. The second was the dire wolf, Fenrir. The third was Hel.

It was prophesied that these three monsters would bring disaster on the gods. "For they are as ferocious as their mother, and as cunning as their father."

Odin sent the gods to gather the vile offspring of Loki and Angrboda and bring them to him.

First he commanded the serpent to be cast into the deeps of the sea and lie there, encircling the earth, until the ends of time. It is said that the god Thor once fished it up, when he was out at sea with the giant Hymir, but just as Thor reached for his hammer to deal it the death blow, Hymir cut the line, and the serpent sank back beneath the waves.

Then Odin threw Hel into Niflheim, to establish her own realm there. While the warriors who die in battle go to Odin or Freya, all those who die of sickness or old age go to Hel. The threshold of her mansion is called the Stumbling Block. No sunlight reaches through that portal. Her walls are draped with Gloom. Her bed is Sickness, her dish is Hunger, her knife is Famine. The glow in her hearth is not fire but Poison.

Then Odin gave thought to the binding of the wolf, Fenrir. He was so fierce that only Tyr, the warrior, dared go close enough to feed him. The gods made a fetter, which they called Leyding, and put it on Fenrir, challenging the wolf to break it. With a shrug of his powerful muscles, the wolf burst free. Next they made a fetter twice as strong, called Dromi; but this, too, the wolf shattered.

So Odin sent Freyr's servant, Skirnir, down to the world of the dwarfs to ask them to make a fetter that would bind the wolf.

They forged it from the sound of a cat's footfall, a woman's beard, a mountain's roots, a bear's sinews, a fish's breath, and a bird's spit. They called it Gleipnir. It was as smooth and supple as a silk ribbon, but as tough and strong as an iron chain.

The Aesir took the wolf to an island in the middle of a lake and showed him Gleipnir. They said, "You have gained great fame by breaking the two fetters we made for you. Now test yourself against this."

Fenrir replied, "How can I gain fame by breaking something so flimsy? There must be some trickery here, and I will not let you put this thing on me."

Odin replied, "If you try to break this ribbon and fail, then clearly you are no threat to the gods, and we will free you."

The wolf still smelled a trap. "Once you have bound me, you may change your mind. I will not refuse your challenge, but let one of you put your hand in my mouth, to show good faith."

The gods looked at one another in dismay. None of them wanted to do this thing. But Tyr bravely put his right hand in the wolf's mouth.

When they put Gleipnir on him, Fenrir struggled to free himself. The harder he tried, the more

tightly the fetter held him. At last, seeing that the gods did not intend to free him as Odin had promised, the wolf snapped his great jaws shut and bit off Tyr's right hand.

The gods left Fenrir bound on the island, until the day of doom. They did not kill him, despite the dark prophecies, because they did not want to stain the holy ground of Asgard with his tainted blood.

THE DEATH OF BALDER

BALDER THE BEAUTIFUL was married to Nanna. Their son, Forseti, was one of the wisest of the gods, and many came to him with their problems and arguments. Balder himself was the only god who had no enemies. Everyone loved him.

So when Balder's sleep began to be disturbed by terrible dreams, all the gods were worried. Night after night, Balder dreamed that he was soon to die.

His father, Odin, rode his horse Sleipnir down the rainbow bridge, all the way to Hel. There he found the walls bedecked with jewels and the venom rivers flowing with gold. Mead was brewing in great cauldrons. "Who is this for?" he asked.

"For Balder," was Hel's cold reply.

At last Balder's mother, Frigg, decided to ask everything in the world to promise not to harm

her son. Fire promised. Water promised. Earth promised. All the birds, the beasts, the plants, the trees promised. No disease would weaken him, no venom would poison him.

When she returned to Asgard, she told Balder that now he was safe and could forget his terrible dreams. Soon Balder felt so secure that the gods made up a new game. Balder would stand in a circle of gods by the well of fate, and they would take turns in throwing stones or weapons at him. However hard they threw, nothing would harm him.

Now Loki, seeing Frigg's son so happy and safe, began to brood on what the gods had done to his children. He thought of Jormungand, at the bottom of the sea; of Hel, in the blighted wastes of Niflheim; and of Fenrir, bound and howling on his lonely island prison. He asked Frigg, in wondering tones, "Did everything in the whole world really promise not to harm Balder?"

She replied, "Yes, except for one small shoot of mistletoe that grows to the west of Valhalla. It was too small to be asked for such a promise."

At once Loki went to the place and plucked that mistletoe.

When he returned, the gods were still enjoying their game, hurling missiles at the laughing Balder. Only Balder's blind brother, Hoder, was standing aside, looking sad.

"Why are you not joining in?" asked Loki.

"I cannot see where Balder is, and even if I could, I have no weapon."

"I will help you aim. Here, take this stick of mistletoe and throw it. You can't be the only one not to take part."

So Hoder took the mistletoe, and Loki guided his hand.

The mistletoe flew straight at Balder, and pierced him to the heart. He fell dead to the ground.

The gods were shocked into silence. They scarcely knew what to do. They could not take revenge on Loki, for none of them dared shed blood in that holy place. They could not help Balder; he was beyond their aid.

Odin sent his son Hermod back down to Hel on Sleipnir, to plead with Hel not to keep Balder, but let him live again.

The other gods brought Balder's body down to the seashore and laid it in his ship, on a funeral pyre. When his wife Nanna saw him lying there, she fell down dead of grief, and she, too, was laid on the pyre.

Odin lit the flame, and Thor hallowed the fire with his hammer, Miollnir. All the gods wept; Freya shed tears of gold.

Meanwhile Hermod took the dark road to Hel, where the souls of the dead flock like flies on a fetid swamp. When he entered its halls, he saw that his brother was already there.

Hermod pleaded with Hel to allow Balder to come back to Asgard. "The whole world weeps for him," he said.

"If that is true," said Hel, "I will allow Balder to return. But the whole world must truly weep."

So Hermod took Hel's message back to Asgard, and Odin and Frigg sent messengers across the world to ask all creation to weep Balder out of Niflheim. Fire wept. Water wept. Earth wept. All plants and creatures, gods, humans, dwarfs, and giants wept.

The messengers returned to Asgard, sure that they had accomplished their task. But on the way home they came to a deserted cave, where they found a giantess sitting, dry-eyed. She said her name was Thokk.

They asked her to weep for Balder, but she replied, "He never wept for me, so I will not weep for him. Let Hel keep him."

So Balder was lost to the gods through the malice of Loki, who had turned spiteful and sly, brooding on the gods' harsh treatment of his children. No one had to tell the grieving Frigg that Thokk, the giantess, was really Loki in disguise, for she knew all fates—even this one that was so hard for her to bear.

THE HUNT FOR LOKI

SOME OF THE LIGHT WENT OUT of life for the gods after Balder's death. Their old, easy fellowship was gone. The rafters of Gladsheim no longer rang with laughter. Sif no longer sang as she combed her golden hair, and Thor journeyed ever further to the east, searching for Loki in the forgotten corners of Jotunheim. Back in Asgard, Odin and Frigg tried vainly to comfort each other.

The sea god Aegir, whose wife Ran catches the souls of drowned sailors in her net, decided to throw a party. "Life must go on," he said. Thor had won Aegir a magic cauldron from the giant Hymir. All Aegir had to do was say, "Cauldron, brew," and it would fill itself with ale. So Aegir and Ran invited all the gods—save Thor, who was still away—to drown their sorrows in ale.

At first the party went well. Everyone tried hard to have fun. Then suddenly the babble of cheerful voices fell away. There was one of those moments of pure silence that sometimes happen at a party. The gods looked up, and there, standing as cool as you like in Aegir's hall, was Loki.

"I claim guest-right," he said. "I'm thirsty. Someone give me a cup of ale."

No one moved.

"I can remember a time, Odin," said Loki, "when you and I were blood brothers. Then you would not have denied me a drink."

Odin turned to his youngest son, Vidar, and said, "Give him ale."

Loki took the cup from Vidar and lifted it to the gods with a twisted smile on his face. "Good health to you all, gods and goddesses."

Bragi snorted in disgust.

Loki turned to him. "Well, perhaps not to you, Bragi. But then, you don't really need me to wish you good health. You protect it well enough yourself. Whenever there's any danger, you usually find something to hide behind, don't you?" Loki put on a simpering tone that mimicked Bragi's gentle voice, "If anyone asks what you are

doing, you always say, 'Oh, I had an idea for a poem.'"

Idun put a loving hand on her husband's arm. "Don't pay any attention, Bragi. Don't give him the satisfaction."

Loki said, "Well, Idun, you'd know all about giving satisfaction. You've flirted all and sundry."

Pure Gefion, the maiden goddess, said, "How can you say such things?"

"Someone explain to Gefion," said Loki in a tired voice.

At that Odin stood up. "You are a fool, Loki, to insult Gefion. Look into your own past if you want someone to rebuke."

"I may not have been perfect," replied Loki, "but at least I never worked men up into a battle frenzy and then deserted them halfway through the battle to let their cowardly opponents win. But you, Odin—that's your idea of fun. As long as lots of them get killed, you don't mind. There's always room in Valhalla for a few more heroes."

Odin said, "Every warrior knows that his luck will run out one day. I have never betrayed a friend."

"And I have never had a friend," said Loki.

Loki proceeded to heap abuse on each of the gods in turn. He uncovered every dirty secret, and shamed them all. It seemed he would never stop.

Loki was just laying into Sif when the distant rumbling of thunder announced the approach of Thor.

"Shut your mouth, Loki, or I will shut it for you," growled Thor from the doorway. "It is a pity you ever managed to untie your lips in the first place."

"I have said what I came to say," replied Loki. "All that's left is to thank Aegir here for his hospitality. It's such a shame that this is the last party you'll ever hold here." And with that, shape-changing Loki turned himself into a living flame and set fire to Aegir's hall. By next morning, all that remained was a few charred timbers and a wrecked cauldron that would never brew ale again.

Loki hid himself from the wrath of the gods. He fled to a remote mountain, where he built himself a house with four doors so that he could keep watch in every direction. During the day he hid in the form of a salmon, in the pool at the foot of a waterfall. At night he sat by his fire, trying to think how the gods could catch him, if they found him.

One night he idly picked up some thread and started to knot it together, making a net, in the way that, ever since, fishers have made their nets. Then he looked to the west, and jumped up in alarm. The gods were coming, for Odin had spied him from his high seat in Asgard.

Loki tossed the net into the fire, and leaped in salmon form all the way down to the pool.

When the gods reached his house, he was gone, leaving no trace. But one-eyed Odin saw the pattern of the net in the ashes of his fire. Realizing it must be for catching fish, he made another net just like it, and the gods took it down to the waterfall.

The first time they threw in the net, Loki escaped by flattening himself between two stones at the bottom of the pool. The second time, he escaped by leaping up the waterfall. But when the gods saw the gleaming curve of a salmon against the spray of plunging water, they knew that they had found their quarry. They took the net to the top of the waterfall, and cast it again. This time, as Loki jumped clear, Thor seized him by the tail. He gripped him so hard that, ever since, salmon have tapered at the tail.

The gods showed no mercy to Loki then. They took him to a cave and bound him across three stones with the entrails of his son, Narfi. Narfi's guts turned into iron chains that bound Loki fast. Then Skadi hung a poisonous snake above Loki's face so that its venom would drip on him. And there they left him, to wait out in anguish the long years until Ragnarok, the twilight of the gods.

But he is not alone. His faithful wife Sigyn sits with him, holding a bowl beneath the snake to catch its venom. When the bowl is full, she has to turn away to empty it. The venom drips into Loki's eyes, and he writhes in agony. Then the whole world shakes.

RAGNAROK

EVEN THE AESIR WILL NOT LIVE FOREVER. Long ago their end was foretold, the twilight of the gods.

A bitter wind will blow at the ruin of the world. It will be a sword age, a wolf age, an ice age. Brother will slay brother; friend will betray friend.

The whole earth will shake itself to pieces. Mountains will fall and seas will rise. Fenrir, Jormungand, and their father, Loki, will be freed from their bonds. Surt of the blazing sword will lead the hordes of Muspell against Asgard; as they ride across the rainbow bridge it will shatter beneath them.

The dread ship Naglfar, which is fashioned from dead people's nails, will be launched at last from Hel; Loki will be its steersman.

The wolf Fenrir will swallow the sun.

Then Heimdall, the watchman of the gods, will blow his horn, and Ragnarok, the last battle, will begin.

Though the gods will fight with all their strength, they will be fighting against the odds. Loki, the cleverest of them all, will be on the side of their enemies. Tyr, the bravest, will be hampered by the loss of his right hand to the wolf, Fenrir.

As for Freyr, he will have no sword at all. For one day Freyr dared to sit on Odin's high seat in Asgard, and looked out over the world. Far away in Jotunheim his eyes were captured by the most beautiful girl he had ever seen. She was Gerd, daughter of the giant Gymir—a girl as lovely as a raindrop or a flame. And Freyr sent his servant Skirnir to Gerd with messages of love and longing, and gave Skirnir his own sword to protect him on the way. So Freyr must face the hordes of Muspell without a sword.

Odin will fight Fenrir, and the wolf will devour him.

Thor will be by his side, but unable to help because he will be struggling with the world serpent, Jormungand. He will slay the serpent, step back nine paces, and fall down dead from

the poison the serpent has spat at him.

It will be left to Vidar to avenge his father Odin's death by killing Fenrir. He will step on the wolf's

lower jaw, with a special shoe made from all the waste pieces that people cut off their shoes at the toe and the heel. Then he will seize Fenrir's upper jaw in his hands, and tear the wolf in two.

Others of the Aesir will fall. Each has their appointed doom.

Freyr will be cut down by Surt with his flaming sword. Tyr will be killed by the evil dog, Garm. Loki and Heimdall will kill each other.

Then Surt will waste the earth with fire; he will set the whole world ablaze.

A NEW BEGINNING

AFTER SURT HAS BURNED THE WORLD, it is said that a new sun will be born, and a new earth will rise from the sea.

To it will come Odin's sons Vidar and Vali, and Thor's sons Modi and Magni, with his hammer, Miollnir. They alone of the gods will have survived Ragnarok.

They will be joined by Balder, released from Hel at last, with his blind brother, Hoder, by his side.

Together they will sit where gold-roofed Asgard used to be, and remember. In the grass they will find the golden chess pieces with which the Aesir used to play, and weep for the glory that has gone.

The world tree shall shelter one man and one woman from Surt's scorching flames. Their names

will be Lif and Lifthrasir, and they will feed on the morning dew.

From them, a new untarnished race of humans will be born, to inherit the new green earth.

WHO'S WHO

PRONUNCIATION: The Viking names can be pronounced as spelled without going too far wrong. I have omitted the "j" in names such as Freyja (Freya), or printed it as "i" as in Miollnir. The "d" in Odin and many other names should properly be pronounced as "th" in them, but there is no harm in substituting a hard "d." "Ei" is pronounced $\bar{a}$ as in late; *"ae" is pronounced like the word* eye.

AEGIR, god of the sea, is married to Ran.

BALDER is Odin's second son, beautiful, just, and loved by all. He is married to Nanna, and their son Forseti is the god of justice.

FREYA is the goddess of fertility, magic, and war, sister of Freyr.

FREYR, brother of Freya, is a god of fertility.

FRIGG, wife of Odin, knows all fates.

GEFION is the goddess of virginity.

GULLVEIG is a witch.

HEIMDALL is the watchman of the gods.

HODER is the blind brother of Balder.

HONIR is the silent god, a companion of Odin.

IDUN, wife of Bragi, god of poetry, guards the apples of life.

KVASIR was made from the spittle of all the gods, and so possessed all their knowledge and wisdom.

LOKI is a frost giant who becomes a god; he was Odin's foster brother. He is married to Sigyn and his offspring include his son Narfi; the eight-legged horse, Sleipnir; the world serpent, Jormungand; the wolf, Fenrir; and Hel, the mistress of Niflheim, the underworld.

MIMIR is the god of wisdom and prophecy.

NIORD, father of Freya and Freyr, marries Skadi, the daughter of the giant Thiassi.

ODIN is the chief of the Aesir, the Norse gods. He is the All-father. With his brothers, Vili and Ve, he created the first man and woman, Ask and Embla, and made the world from the body of the giant Ymir. From Ymir's body also come the frost giants, rock giants, and dwarfs. Odin is married to Frigg. His ravens, Huginn (Thought) and Muninn (Memory), tell him everything that happens in the world. His horse is the eight-legged Sleipnir. He is a god of war and welcomes the spirits of warriors to the halls of Valhalla. His sons include Vidar and Vali. He disguises himself as Bolverk.

SURT will lead the armies of Muspell against the gods in the last battle, Ragnarok.

SUTTUNG, a giant, wins the mead of poetry from the murderous dwarfs Fialar and Galar. His father was Gilling and his daughter is Gunnlod.

THIALFI and his sister Roskva, are bond servants of Thor.

THOR is Odin's first son, god of thunder. His weapon is the hammer, Miollnir, forged by the dwarfs Brokk and Eitri, and stolen by the giant Hymir. He is married to Sif; their sons are Modi and Magni.

TYR is a god of battle.

UTGARD-LOKI is king of the giants. He also calls himself Skrymir, and his servants include Elli (Old Age), Hugi (Thought), and Logi (Flame).

AFTERWORD

THE NORSE GODS, the Aesir, were the gods of the Vikings, the warlike adventurers who thrived in Scandinavia from around A.D. 800 to A.D. 1100. The Vikings were an extraordinary people, who combined farming and lawmaking with ferocious treasure-hunting raids and daring voyages of discovery. Leif the Lucky, son of Erik the Red, who discovered Greenland, voyaged as far as North America, which he named Vinland.

The Viking gods had their origins in the Germanic gods of Northern Europe, but developed to suit the particular nature of the Vikings. The war between the Aesir and the Vanir shows the old fertility gods submitting to the gods of war; in Norse mythology even the chief fertility deity, Freyr, is male.

Our sources of information about these Viking gods are few and scattered. The main stories are cryptically expressed in the mythological verses known as the *Elder* or *Poetic Edda*, and told more plainly by the Icelander Snorri Sturluson in his *Edda*, also known as the *Younger* or *Prose Edda*. Snorri's work was essentially a study of Viking poetry, and the word *Edda* can be translated as "poetics." By the time he was writing—about A.D. 1300—the Viking gods had been eclipsed by Christianity, and Icelandic poets could no longer understand the mythological allusions in earlier poetry without such a guide.

Without Snorri, our understanding of the Viking gods would be vague. It seems that, even though he was writing from a Christian viewpoint, he represented the myths clearly and fairly, but there are obvious gaps. For instance, Snorri says that the Asyniur, the goddesses, are just as holy and powerful as the gods, the Aesir, but apart from Frigg and Freya we hardly know anything about them. That the goddesses do not come much into the stories does not mean that they were not worshiped, but rather that the stories were shaped from a male perspective.

An eleventh-century account of the Viking temple at Uppsala tells us that the three most important gods were Odin, Thor, and Freyr, and describes how they were worshiped in the form of statues, and how sacrifices of dogs, horses, and men were made to them. Another source describes the statue of Thor in the temple at Thrandheim:

> Thor sat in the middle. He was the most highly honored. He was huge, and all adorned with gold and silver. Thor was arranged to sit in a chariot; he was very splendid. There were goats, two of them, harnessed in front of him, very well wrought. Both car and goats ran on wheels. The rope round the horns was of twisted silver, and the whole was worked with extremely fine craftsmanship.

The temple-worship of these male gods may have been matched by less formal rituals invoking the goddesses. Freya, Freyr's sister and sometime consort, is linked with the seeresses known as *volva*, who practiced a kind of shamanism in Viking Scandinavia; while men took their oaths over Thor's arm ring in the temple, women swore to the goddess Var.

Although widespread belief in Odin, Thor, and

their fellows survived at least into the twelfth century—and Snorri Sturluson describes Freya as "still living," implying that her worship had not entirely died out—the Viking religion gave way to Christianity throughout Scandinavia. The old gods were ousted for all kinds of reasons, including practical ones of trade and politics. By A.D. 1100 Denmark and Norway were largely Christianized, and Sweden followed over the next century.

For a time, of course, the two religions survived side by side. There must have been many Norsemen such as Helgi the Skinny who "believed in Christ, but prayed to Thor on sea journeys and in tough situations." The binding of Loki and the suffering of Odin on Yggdrasil could be interpreted in Christian terms, and scenes from Norse mythology and Christian belief intermingle, for instance, on a stone cross in the churchyard at Gosforth in Cumbria, England.

Though the Viking gods are no longer worshiped, their rich mythology lives on. And we remember them, for their names survive in our days of the week: Tuesday (Tiw, or Tyr's day), Wednesday (Woden, or Odin's day), Thursday (Thor's day), and Friday (Frigg's day).

SUGGESTED READINGS

For Children:

Daly, Kathleen N. *Norse Mythology A to Z: A Young Reader's Companion.* New York and Oxford: Facts on File, 1991.

MacDonald, Fiona. *Vikings.* New York: Barrons, 1992, and Oxford: Oxford University Press, 1992.

Margeson, Susan M. *Viking.* New York: Knopf, 1994, and London: Dorling Kindersley, 1994.

Nicholson, Robert, and Claire Watts. *The Vikings: Facts, Stories, and Activities.* New York and Philadelphia: Chelsea Juniors, 1994.

Philip, Neil. *The Illustrated Book of Myths.* London, New York, and Stuttgart: Dorling Kindersley, 1995.

Treece, Henry. *The Viking Saga.* London: Puffin, 1985. Contains *Viking's Dawn.* New York; Phillips, 1956; *The Road to Miklagard.* New York: Phillips, 1957; and *Viking's Sunset.* New York; Criterion, 1961

Treece, Henry. *Vinland the Good.* London: Bodley Head, 1967; as *Westward to Vinland.* New York: Phillips, 1967.

For Adults:

Elliott, Ralph W. V. *Runes.* 2nd ed. Manchester: Manchester University Press, and New York: St. Martin's Press, 1989.

Ellis-Davidson, H. R. *Gods and Myths of Northern Europe.* Harmondsworth and Baltimore: Penguin Books, 1964.

Graham-Campbell, James, et al. *Cultural Atlas of the Viking World.* New York and Oxford: Facts on File, 1994.

Graham-Campbell, James, and Dafydd Kidd. *The Vikings.* London: British Museum Publications, 1980.

Haywood, John. *The Penguin Historical Atlas of the Vikings.* London and New York: Penguin Books, 1995.

Jesche, Judith. *Women in the Viking Age.* Woodbridge, Suffolk, and Rochester, New York: Boydell Press, 1991.

Roesdahl, Else. *The Vikings.* London and New York: Penguin Books, 1992.

Wahlgren, Erik. *The Vikings and America.* London: Thames and Hudson, 1986.

SOURCES

Auden, W. H., and Paul B. Taylor. *Norse Poems.* London: Athlone Press, 1981.
Crossley-Holland, Kevin. *The Norse Myths.* London: André Deutsch, 1980.
Hollander, Lee, trans. *The Poetic Edda.* Austin: University of Texas Press, 1969.
Sturluson, Snorri. *Edda,* translated and introduced by Anthony Faulkes. London: J. M. Dent, and Rutland, Vermont: Charles E. Tuttle, 1987.